Whopper

A Novel

For Readers Ages 9–12

Happy reading!

Idella Bodie

OTHER BOOKS BY IDELLA BODIE

Ghost in the Capitol

Ghost Tales for Retelling

A Hunt for Life's Extras:
The Story of Archibald Rutledge

The Mystery of Edisto Island

The Mystery of the Pirate's Treasure

The Secret of Telfair Inn

South Carolina Women

Stranded!

Trouble at Star Fort

Whopper

A Novel by
Idella Bodie

Illustrated by
Gay Haff Kovach

Sandlapper Publishing, Inc.

To Jason, whose imagination
sometimes gets him into
trouble

Copyright © 1989 by Sandlapper Publishing, Inc.
Copyright © 1995 by Idella Bodie

First printing, 1989
Second printing, 1995

MANUFACTURED IN THE UNITED STATES OF AMERICA

Published by Sandlapper Publishing Co., Inc.
Orangeburg, South Carolina

Library of Congress Cataloging in Publication Data

Bodie, Idella.
   Whopper

   Summary: Howie's fabricated stories get him in
trouble at school and earn him the nickname "Whopper."
   [1. Honesty—Fiction. 2. Behavior—Fiction.
3. Schools—Fiction] I. Kovach, Gay Haff, ill.
II. Title.
PZ7.B63525Wh 1989   [Fic]   88-36243
ISBN 0-87844-091-7
ISBN 0-87844-086-0 (pbk.)

Contents

When I was a little boy,
they called me a liar;
but now that I'm grown up,
they call me a writer.
        —Isaac Bashevis Singer

1
School!

Boring. Boring.

Nothing in the whole world could be more boring than school—especially Miss Lail's fifth grade class. It was the pits, the plain old boring pits.

As if school wasn't bad enough by itself, Howie thought, here he was in the big old shadowy hallway of Ridgeville Elementary, writing for punishment.

157. I must not tell lies.
158. I must not tell lies.

Out of the corner of his eye he caught movement down the hall. A boy was leaving the third grade classroom with a bathroom pass in his hand. The light from the end of the hall made the boy a moving black form. Howie heard a *tick, tick*. His heart beat faster. Maybe it wasn't the bathroom pass he was carrying after all. Maybe he was going to plant a bomb in the boys' bathroom.

Suddenly Miss Lail appeared in the doorway. Howie felt her stare. It pierced the excitement of the moment, causing his slightly lifted spirits to go *splat* like a wet washcloth.

Miss Lail had been good and mad when she plopped a desk outside their classroom and put him in it.

"You have gone too far this time, Howard McDougal," she had said, pushing her glasses up on her nose and pressing her lips together in that thin straight line Howie knew so well.

Long before he got in her class, Howie had heard that there was no use wasting your breath if Miss Lail said do something.

Yep, his dad had told him all about her. She had been his teacher, too.

Howie shook his hand to get the cramps out of his fingers. Only three weeks into the school year, and it seemed like forever. He closed and opened his hand. It would never feel normal again.

He propped his chin on his hand and looked up at the transom, a sort of window panel above the door across the hall. Like the transoms for all the other rooms in the high-ceilinged corridor, it was open to circulate air. All in a moment the glass panel seemed to float before Howie's eyes. Like a magic carpet it drifted down, gathered him aboard, swished down the hall and out the great oak door into the silvery sky. Howie could feel the sunshine as he sailed above his small Southern hometown en route to Miami, Florida, and his grandmother, Mamma Grace. Only hours earlier he had been wishing she hadn't remarried and moved away from Ridgeville, but now he was being swirled through the sweet-smelling air to her, and they could play games again. Better yet, he could skip school now and then with a stomachache, and she could take care of him.

Somewhere a door slammed with the clicking of a heavy lock. Howie looked up from the desk in the hallway to see the principal, Mr. Derrick, moving toward him in his fast-stepping, businesslike way.

"Well, Howard," he said in passing, "I certainly hope you have learned your lesson."

"Yessir," Howie mumbled to his back and hunkered down once again over his page.

If only he was *am-bi*—what was that word? He and his dad had talked about it just the other day when they were pitching ball. Howie had tried to throw with his left hand, but it just wouldn't work. His father had laughed.

"If you want to be *am-bi-dex-trous*"—that was it—*ambidextrous*—he had said, "you have to work at it."

It was too bad he wasn't ambidextrous so he could give his right hand a rest. But trying to practice now would be too messy, and Miss Lail would never stand for that. His paper was already bad enough. His letters wouldn't go the same way, and in some places eraser smudges had torn holes all the way through the paper.

Howie let out a long sigh and picked up his pencil. He couldn't stand writing the same thing over and over. Besides, he liked big words like ambidextrous that meant simple things.

159. I must not tell lies.
160. I must not tell lies.

While he wrote, Howie kept one ear tuned to the classroom. He could hear Miss Lail's voice slicing the air like a butcher's cleaver. She was still mad. He could tell. She never yelled when she got angry. Instead of busting loose, she held her body as straight as a yardstick, and she pronounced every word extra carefully. Her voice reminded Howie of a firecracker about to go off.

Nope, Miss Lail wasn't a shouter like that third grade teacher down the hall. Howie could hear her letting her class have it right now.

Inside his classroom, tattletale Carolyn McClain was answering all Miss Lail's questions. Because the name *McClain* came right before *McDougal* in the alphabet, Howie had sat behind Carolyn every single year since first grade. That girl made him sick to his stomach—just like all this writing of the same thing over and over.

Suddenly an idea popped into his head.

He would write each word all the way down the page and then come back up for the next one. That way he wouldn't have to think about what the words said.

That Carolyn. It was all her fault. If only she was a boy for just one day, Howie would give her a black eye. Or better yet, he would punch her in her fat stomach. This stupid writing was really all her fault. She was always

4

161. ♪
162. ♪
163. ♪
164. ♪
165. ♪

sneaking around listening and then tattling to the teacher.

It had all started this morning when Howie was coming to school. Around by the lunchroom he had seen the delivery man dashing in and out of his milk truck, carrying trays of half-pint milk cartons into the lunchroom the way he always did. Only today he didn't look like the man who usually brought the milk to the school. He wasn't wearing his red-and-white striped Royal Dairy uniform. Instead he wore a strange-looking coat with a hood on it. The weather wasn't cool enough for that.

No sirree, it hadn't taken Howie long to figure out what was going on. *This guy was involved in a coverup plot to overthrow their town, and he was starting with the kids.* He had managed to slip something into their milk before it was packaged at Royal's Dairy, and shortly after lunch they'd all be dropping like flies.

Howie had to admit that it did sound a bit strange when he whispered, "Don't drink your milk!" to his best friend

Tommy and the other fellows around him at the lunch table. But somebody would have to be around when the reporters from the newspapers came out to cover the story.

Before Howie knew what was happening, old eavesdropping Carolyn had hopped up from her place and run alongside the table, her curls going *boing, boing* as she moved. She prissed up to Miss Lail, leaned over and whispered something behind her hand.

Carolyn hadn't even straightened up, when Howie felt

Miss Lail's stare boring a hole in him.

One of the boys yelled out, "You've done it this time, Howie!"

Then somebody else hollered, "That's Howie's biggest whopper yet!"

Miss Lail jumped up like a puppet with its strings being pulled. Nearly running into some snaky-looking plants hanging from the ceiling, she headed straight toward Howie. The veins in her neck looked like the plastic worms in a fishing tackle box.

Somebody called out, "Whopper, Whopper, shoots off his top like a corn popper!"

A chubby girl in a red blouse laughed like a duck quacking. In no time at all the lunch table was in an uproar, and as if by magic the principal appeared and glowered over them. In the confusion, Howie caught a glimpse of Miss Lail. Her spectacles framed brown dots that looked right through to his soul. Miss Lail's children always behaved in the lunchroom. She saw to it that they did. All of a sudden the mashed potatoes Howie had eaten felt like a heavy glob in his stomach.

Now over an hour later, here he sat in the hallway writing this dumb thing. It wasn't fair. Worse still, that stinking old Carolyn didn't even get fussed at for hopping up from the lunch table without permission. She knew Miss Lail had said nobody was to get up and come to her unless the person next to him had died. Carolyn ought to have to write, "I must not be a tattletale," one thousand times.

Howie worked the word *not* down the page before he

7

stopped again to rub his hand. Underneath his anger lay the thought of what one of the fellows at the lunch table had said—"the biggest *whopper* of all." Somebody else had picked it up. "Whopper," they had called him.

And Tommy. Even his best friend Tommy was against him. Suddenly Howie's sigh turned into a groan. Nobody in the whole school liked him any more.

Then for some reason Howie thought about his hamster, Friday. He would be sniffing around the corners of his cage about now, waiting for Howie to come home from school. At least he had a friend in Friday.

But before Howie could work his feelings into a happier state, Miss Lail was at the door motioning for him to come inside.

2
Big Trouble

Inside the classroom Howie saw that Miss Lail had the class standing like clothespins on a line. He hardly had time to shove his books in his bag and hoist it on his back before Miss Lail stepped closer to him, crooked her finger, and pointed toward the small space in front of Carolyn.

Ugh! Standing beside Carolyn McClain—even for a minute—was worse than writing *"I must not tell lies."*

Why his class had to line up to be dismissed he'd never understand. Most of the teachers didn't make their kids stand in line. But leave it up to good old Miss Lail to be the strictest one.

The bell clanged, and "Miss Lail's line" moved out, broke up, and was caught up in the shouts and jostles of the hallway. Howie heard the other kids' shoes slap the wooden floor as they dashed past him.

Outside, the smell of fresh air with a tinge of fall washed over him. He shaded his eyes against the sun, which was hanging half way down the sky, and skimmed the playground looking for Tommy. Finally he spotted him standing down near the water fountain with a lively bunch of kids. When they caught sight of Howie, a girl pointed and yelled, "There he is!" A boy Howie didn't recognize shouted "Liar! Liar! Your pants are on fire!" Others picked up the chant and peals of laughter rang in the air.

Howie turned toward the bus ramp, but not before he caught sight of Tommy's face. Even from a distance he could see the big grin spread all over it. Well, let him side with the others against his best friend. Howie didn't care. He moved along the chain link fence, stuck out his hand, and listened to the sound of his fingers plunking across the cold metal. That was just the way he felt—just like a dull old *plunk*.

"Hey, Howie! Wait up!" A sixth grader, his books dangling from a strap, took giant steps to catch up with him. "I heard you spaced out Old Lady Lail today," the boy said. His voice sounded as if he were kidding, but Howie didn't respond.

"*Hmmm*," he mumbled in answer and climbed onto the yellow school bus. He didn't want to think about the lunchroom episode or about Miss Lail. Somehow she always made him think of long division, with all your work showing.

Just as he stuck his head above the rail guarding the front seat, somebody from the back of the bus yelled, "Hey, Howie, tell us about the poisoned milk."

"Yeah, 'Whopper,'" chimed another. "That's the best one I've heard yet."

Howie leaned over, slipped his book-bag strap off his

shoulder, and let the weight of the books pull him down in the window seat behind the driver. He would ignore them—all of them. He concentrated all his energy on ignoring everything—even the banter of the fellows in the back of the bus who were playing "keep-away" with some little kid's cap. He would wash his mind of everything having to do with school, and most especially the "I must not tell lies" paper in his book bag that he had to finish. He'd probably never get to 500—probably not even if he lived to be a hundred, much less by Friday.

Out of the corner of his eye he could see monkeylike arms dangling out of the bus windows.

"Okay!" The boom of the driver's voice nearly burst Howie's eardrums. "Settle down right this minute, or I'm reporting you all to the principal!"

Howie sucked in a deep breath, shrugged his shoulders, and looked out the window. Across from the schoolyard, railroad tracks curved away into nothingness. One of these days he would hop a freight train and be a hobo. He'd do some really exciting things then. Maybe he'd even take Friday along.

A locomotive chugged around the bend, drowning out the noise of the bus. Suddenly Howie was the engineer. He pulled the whistle and a *"Whoo—whooooooo . . . "* pierced the air. The noise spoke of prairies and rivers, of cowboys riding over mountain trails, of campfires and staying up late at night under the stars.

School was a million miles away—no long division, no Miss Lail, no Carolyn, no stupid writing the same thing

over and over. And best of all, Howie's friend Tommy grinned at him over an evening campfire.

A loud screech, unlike the rails of his train, sounded in Howie's ears. He looked up to see his corner bus stop. As he tumbled out of the big yellow bus along with several little kids who lived down a side street from him, a voice called, "Bye, Whopper."

"Bug off, Shrimp!" Howie heard himself say. With a twinge of guilt he watched the kid who had called out sprint for his street. Enough was enough.

Once on the sidewalk, Howie felt as if the bottom of his shoes had been plastered with glue. His notebook with the unfinished business lay heavy in his bag. He sighed and cast a weary look toward the Johnsons' yard. Sometimes, when he felt like it, he walked around the block to keep from going by those neighbors' house.

The day Mrs. Johnson accused him, in her high thin voice, of throwing the grape icy cup on her lawn was fresh in his mind. Her cold, bony fingers had grabbed him by his shirt collar and sent shivers down his back. He had tried to tell her that the motorcycle rider with the yellow helmet must have flung the cup into her yard, but she just kept squawking—like that mamma jay in Howie's back-yard squawked when he walked under the apple tree where her nest was.

Besides, he just plain didn't like the Johnsons' yard. Mr. Johnson took his electric clippers and shaped all the trees and bushes the way he wanted them, not the way God intended them to be. Some of the shrubs ended up with

13

little round balls on top. They looked for all the world like newly clipped poodles.

As Howie neared his own back door, a good smell—maybe chocolate chip cookies—reached him. A cold glass of milk with some warm cookies would sure taste good.

Just as he reached out to let himself in, the screen door popped open and almost hit him in the face. His mother stood in the door, glaring at him.

"Get in here and go straight to your room, young man. I'm fed up with those whoppers you're telling."

"Oh, no," Howie groaned under his breath as he headed toward his room. The bad news had beat him home, and his mom was on their side, too.

"Carolyn's mother," she yelled to his back, "just called me about the trouble you caused at school today."

3
The Showdown

Howie flung his book bag on the floor and fell backward across his bed. His mom's voice was trembling, and she had seemed near tears when she shoved him in his room and slammed the door. But she definitely wasn't sad like the time when Miss Lail reported Howie wasn't doing his homework. If she cried this time, it would be from anger. Her face had been all fiery looking.

Howie could hear her dialing the phone. She was probably calling his dad and Miss Lail and Mr. Derrick and goodness knows who all. Now everybody on earth was going to be mad with him—except maybe Mamma Grace. She would probably say, "They're all just trying to make a mountain out of a mole hill."

Mamma Grace. She sure fouled things up when she let that old Mr. Spencer talk her into marrying him. But Howie couldn't really blame him, even if he did look like a tub. Mamma Grace was fun. He missed her.

Howie rubbed his stomach. It felt all hollow. He thought about the cookies on the kitchen counter. He could still smell the warm chocolate. Life was so unfair.

He turned his head to see Friday in his cage against the wall. Even his hamster looked all down in the dumps—like somebody had died. Howie thought about taking his pet out of the cage for a little exercise, but on second thought he knew he'd better not take the chance just now. If Friday got loose in the house, his mom would really be mad. She didn't like Friday touching her. The only thing she had ever liked about him was his name. When they got Friday from a pet shop that was going out of business, Howie heard that the hamsters that were left would go to the university lab for experiments. Because of that, Howie's dad suggested the name Friday. After all, Howie had rescued his hamster from a terrible fate just the way Robinson Crusoe had saved his man Friday.

Howie had heard his mom telling some of her friends about his hamster's name. All the same, she just didn't have any use for Friday. Most of the time she called him "that rat." At least she did save raw vegetables for him, and Howie was glad for that. He'd read that if hamsters had only soft foods, their front teeth would grow so long they couldn't close their mouths. Just for good measure, he kept twigs in Friday's cage for him to gnaw on.

He leaned his head back and studied the sky outside his window. It looked all peculiar. A big gray blob of a cloud chased some little ones over the top of the silver maple, making it change colors. One second it was silver; the next, green. Howie bet those leaves never got bored. They could be different all the time. That's what he'd like to do—be different people. He'd like to be a skin diver and find treasure ships—or maybe invent a space ship that would find a tenth planet, somewhere beyond the specks of blue peeking between the maple leaves.

The sound of his father's voice broke into his thoughts. Howie jumped up. What was Dad doing home this early? His mom had phoned him. Had she cried on the phone? He didn't like having his parents upset with him. He edged toward the door and put his ear against it.

"Now, Margaret," his dad was saying. "Just calm down. I thought something much worse had happened, the way you sounded over the phone."

"Worse?" his mother sobbed. "Don't you see what's happening? All the kids at school are telling their parents our son tells lies. We'll be the laughing stock—*along with Howard.*"

His mom was right. All the kids at the water fountain had laughed at him.

"Well," he heard his dad respond, strong and clear, through the closed door, "you can call up your mother and thank her for that."

Howie stiffened. His dad sounded mad—real mad.

"My mother?" Mom had stopped crying. Howie could tell.

"That's right," his father shot back. *"Your mother.* And you can tell her all that 'let's pretend' junk she used to carry on with him has backfired."

"That's not fair, Howard!" His mom was screaming now.

Howie felt dizzy. He crawled toward his bed and pulled himself up. He'd never heard his parents fight like that before, and it was all over him. They were even fighting about Mamma Grace.

For a split second Howie felt better. Thinking of Mamma Grace always made him feel good. He thought of the trips they used to take—well, not *really take*, but sort of. They went places in their imaginations.

Once she made a Black Forest cake, and the two of them had to travel to Germany before they could eat any. Mamma Grace had talked in German. If Howie said anything in English, she raised her eyebrows and shook her head to show she didn't understand him. He kept saying the same thing over and over, and every time she would do the same. They had ended up laughing and laughing, and then Mamma Grace had read him "The Pied Piper of Hamelin," a German legend. Howie wished he could make all the kids at school who laughed at him follow him to a river so he could drown them, the way the Pied Piper had done. That would show them.

With another warm rush of feeling he remembered the times when he was little, and he used to stay overnight with Mamma Grace. She had let Willie, Howie's imaginary friend, sleep in the room with him so he wouldn't be scared of the dark. And once, when he wouldn't eat his vegetables, she almost fed them to Willie.

Howie let out a long shuddery sigh. If only Mamma Grace hadn't gone and married again and moved to Florida.

He tried thinking of the spelling bee he had won last year. That usually made him feel better.

Things had gotten quiet in the rest of the house. Obviously his parents weren't going to let him out of here any time soon. In fact, he wasn't even sure he wanted to be let out—not with the mood they were in. Howie got up and plundered through his chest of drawers like a robber. He turned up an old yo-yo with no string, four jacks, a Sucret box with some sharks' teeth, and an old fluteophone left over from fourth grade music class. He put it to his lips and then stopped short of blowing into it. He dared not play it now.

A prisoner in his own home—that's what he was. He was going to end up at the funny farm if this kept up.

Back on his bed, he tried twiddling his thumbs. It was harder than it looked—keeping your fingers clasped while you made one thumb circle the other. Once you got the hang of it, it was super boring. Even more boring than being plain old bored from doing nothing.

He tried closing one eye. It did give him a different view of his room. The banner on his wall from Disney World took on the shape of a pirate's knife. He covered both his eyes with his hands, and then, for some unknown reason, he was on the playground at school. Carolyn, with her curls still bouncing like springs, was chasing him. Her sing-song voice whined:

"Howie's a whopper. Howie's a whopper."

In his mind's eye he turned and let her almost catch up with him, and then he reached down for a rock and threw it straight at her fat stomach. To his amazement the rock took off in slow motion, and then right before his eyes the rock puffed up and swallowed Carolyn.

Howie opened his eyes and sat up. What he had just seen hadn't really happened. He wished it had. But it had all seemed so real.

Suddenly his thoughts were as jumbled as the numbers before a bingo game. What he had seen had been a daydream. But how could he help it if his mind kept imagining things? At least it gave a little life to dull old Ridgeville.

Still, he hated making his parents unhappy. And as much as he hated to admit it, he did want the kids at school to be friends with him, especially Tommy. The trouble was, nobody understood him. How could they, when he really didn't understand himself? How, he wondered, did people keep their minds from thinking of things they didn't plan to think about?

Oh, well, he might be mixed up on some things, but one thing was as clear as his window pane—they were all against him.

With a new burst of energy Howie scooted over to the edge of his bed and let his head hang backward over the side. He would let all the blood rush to his head and die. Then maybe they'd all be sorry—the whole lot of them.

In no time at all his head began to feel sort of blown up and his eyes felt strange, like they were bulging out the way spiders' eyes sit on their heads.

Howie lay unmoving. He listened for sounds from the other parts of the house. This was the longest time his mom had ever left him to be punished without coming in to talk about it. His ear itched, but he wouldn't move to scratch it. He listened even harder. Not a sound. Had they gone out and left him?

Thump. Thump. His heart pounded. His arms tingled.

His mom wasn't coming.

Finally the door creaked open.

"Son," his father said, "come in the den. Your mother and I want to talk to you."

4
Punishment

After the blowup between his parents, Howie had expected the worst, but lucky for him it didn't turn out that way.

Instead, his mom just looked like he remembered their old lab, Chester, looking when he had a tick on him. Howie wished they still had Chester, but he was old—even older than Howie—when they had to have him put to sleep. He was almost blind, had arthritis, and practically all his teeth had rotted. They'd been mushing up his food for a long time when he got the kidney infection. The vet said he just couldn't make it any longer. Howie had felt so sad. That was why his mom had let him get Friday.

Anyway, Howie's dad had done most of the talking—including telling him that he was grounded for the rest of the week.

Howie's head still felt a little oozy from having all his blood rush to it; but when he heard that, he managed to say, "But holy cow, Dad, it's only Monday."

That started both his parents up again with how lucky

he was to have Miss Lail for a teacher and how ashamed he ought to be.

No leaving his yard. No TV. No riding his bicycle. No telephone calls. No nothing for a whole week.

Adults just didn't understand anything. Of that Howie was sure. He wished he had just kept hanging his head off the bed.

He wasn't quite sure how he did it, but he managed to get through the rest of the day. He lay on his bed and did his homework. He looked at the chapter in his science book on snakes and mice and lizards and stuff until he got a crick in his neck. He was working it out when he remembered the book of Greek myths Mamma Grace had given him. It was in his closet on the shelf with some other books. He pulled it down and leafed through it until he found the story of Achilles. He liked the way Achilles' mother had dipped him in the Styx River when he was a baby, to try to make him live forever. Because she was immortal, she wanted her son to be.

Afterward, Howie made certain his door was tightly closed and let Friday out of his cage to run around the room. He listened to the sounds of the house and watched through his window as the silver leaves of the maple grew purple and then black with the evening light.

And after an almost silent supper, he took the dreaded "I must not tell lies" paper out of his book and wrote up to 422.

Tuesday morning on the school bus, Howie faced the same laughing taunts of "Whopper." His legs felt like squashed bananas as he dropped himself down the bus steps and headed toward the classroom building.

Much to his surprise, Tommy was waiting for him by the front door.

"I tried to call you last night," he said, "but your mom said—"

"Yeah, I know." Howie's voice sounded as rejected as he felt.

"How long did you get?"

"Till Friday."

Tommy let out a whistle. "That's rotten."

"Yeah . . . "

"But—" Tommy pushed the toe of his shoe in the dirt. "Well—why'd you go and tell such a dumb thing anyway?"

Howie swallowed. His throat felt as dry as the dust Tommy stirred up with his shoe. Somebody behind him laughed and when Howie turned, a boy named Eddie pushed Fat Jake into him.

Enough was enough. Howie's Irish temper sent a rush of blood through his head.

"Hey!" he shouted. "Watch out what you're doing, Pie Face."

The morning bell cut across the hubbub, and Howie felt himself moving with the crowd toward another day of torture.

Why should he care if the kids didn't like him any more? It would serve them all right if he never spoke to any of them again. The only thing left for him to do was to become a hermit. He would wear old clothes with patches and grow a beard and let his hair grow long and live on the edge of town in a falling-down shack. He could see his mother now—bringing him bowls of gruel and begging him not to ruin his health.

All morning Carolyn swished around the classroom with that icky little grin on her face, and Tommy whispered to Brent who sat behind him. Howie plunked his geography book down extra hard. He knew now how Philip Nolan felt. They had read about his being sent out to sea to become a man without a country.

As usual the class had plenty of seat work. It started while Miss Lail collected lunch money. First there were word problems in math and then sentences with the spelling words. "We are hard workers," Miss Lail kept repeating as she stalked the aisles. "We are *very* hard workers." She sounded like a stuck recorder. Afterward they did the states and capitals and then read aloud in their science books. Howie couldn't stand the way some of his classmates read in slow motion. It drove him up the wall.

As often as he thought he could get away with it, he got up to trim his pencil. At least he could look out the window. Now and then he could see somebody walking toward the teachers' parking lot. It was too bad his room wasn't on the side with the playground. Then he could look down on the little kids as they chased each other or wrestled on the ground. The problem was his pencil—it didn't take many trips to grind it down to a nub.

During social studies, Carolyn kept sticking her hand

up to answer questions and jiggling to get Miss Lail to call on her. Cripes, how he hated sitting behind that girl.

When Miss Lail turned to the chalkboard, he took a straight pin he'd found on the floor and stuck it through the skin on his thumb. Then he reached around and held his hand in front of Carolyn's face.

"Howie McDougal," Carolyn whispered out of the corner of her mouth, "you're gross." But for once she didn't tattle.

On Wednesday, just after music, Howie got a humongous case of hiccups. Everybody started laughing, and for a fleeting moment it felt like old times.

"Howard," Miss Lail said, "you are excused to get a drink of water—*and hurry back.*"

That woman, thought Howie, could stare down a snake.

Every day was the same boring one as the next. Stay in at recess and do the punishment work. Mope around at home doing homework and as much of the "I must not tell lies" as he could stand. Only the Greek mythology book had saved his sanity. He liked the way Ulysses outsmarted the Cyclops by blinding the one-eyed giant and then telling him his name was "Nobody." No wonder Athena, the goddess of wisdom, liked Ulysses so much. He was a smart hero.

When Thursday finally came, Howie tried to get his spirits up. He was "over the hump," as grownups liked to say about getting through the week. But just as the others lined up for recess, Miss Lail's curt voice flattened his hopes like a punctured balloon.

"Howard," she said, "because you have dilly-dallied on

your punishment work, I am doubling the assignment. All of it is due Friday."

Howie heard a little voice in him crying, "But you can't do that. Tomorrow is Friday." But the little voice never got any louder. Maybe it knew Miss Lail could do anything she pleased. It was important, she went on, to be punctual with all work—punishment work or homework.

While Howie wrote, Miss Lail sat at her desk and opened and closed drawers and bounced stacks of papers to even them up before capturing them with a rubber band. Occasionally she squeaked chalk across the board. Once Howie thought of asking her if he could write some of his "I must not tell lies" on the board to break the monotony. But when he looked at her she seemed to grow taller, and all of a sudden Howie felt like Jack waiting for the giant to find him in the kettle.

The recess break was only fifteen minutes, so Howie couldn't get much done, especially with his hand cramping. Even so, time dragged. Outside he could hear his classmates shouting in fun.

Oh, well, he reasoned, even if he had gotten to go out, no one would play with him. Worst of all, Tommy didn't seem to miss him. He came back in each day from the break all laughing and sweating from playing kickball.

As Tommy passed by Howie's desk, he asked, "How's it going, Whopper?"

"Awh, kiss your elbow," Howie snapped back, "and turn into a girl."

By the time he got to go to recess again, everybody would

have forgotten all about him. Life was moving on around him.

Howie felt so miserable that he wanted everyone else to feel that way too. When Miss Lail asked Bill Jacobs a question in science, Howie whispered the very opposite answer to him and Bill repeated it. The class laughed and Bill's face turned red.

"Howie told me to say that," Bill sputtered apologetically.

Howie almost felt like laughing. Bill was a stupid nut to repeat what Howie had fed him without believing it.

"William," Miss Lail was saying, "Howard is *not* the teacher." Then as an afterthought she added, "Howard, would you like to come up in front of the class and be the teacher?"

Silence hung in the air as Miss Lail waited for the answer she knew she would get.

"No, Ma'am," Howie answered, feeling like a traitor to his conscience.

Miss Lail continued her stare for good measure, pursed her lips, and looked away.

Bill glared at Howie, and Howie wrinkled up his face in a "You-can't-win-'em-all" manner. Could he help it if Miss Lail had absolutely no sense of humor?

After lunch—at least he was allowed to eat, even if it was lunchroom food—Howie tried hard to get his spirits up. But gloom and doom pressed them down, until Miss Lail called on Kaney Smoots for his "dramatic book report."

Kaney stood before the class with his feet spread apart like a captain on a ship. He was Robinson Crusoe. Putting his hand up to shade his eyes from the ocean's glare, he scanned the seas for a sign of a sail. Howie couldn't help thinking that if Kaney were really lost on a desert island, he wouldn't have to worry about being eaten by cannibals. They'd probably think his freckles were some strange disease they would catch if they swallowed him.

All of a sudden Howie laughed out loud.

"Howard!" Miss Lail's voice cut across his laughter and silence hung like a threat.

Howie did his best to put on a sad expression, like the one he had worn when Chester was put to sleep. "I'm sorry, Miss Lail, but I thought of something funny."

"Well, there's nothing funny in this report, young man," she retorted, "and I would advise you to listen."

Under ordinary circumstances Howie would have asked to tell the class about Friday when Kaney sat down, but nobody wanted him to say anything—least of all Miss Lail. Howie thought of throwing up. You automatically got to go home for the rest of the day when that happened. But with no TV it wouldn't be worth the humiliation.

When three o'clock finally did come and Howie got out of the classroom, he felt disoriented, like an astronaut just climbing off a space shuttle.

On the way to the bus he lashed out at everyone around him before they had a chance to taunt him and call him "Whopper."

He worked at pretending he was the only one riding the bus; and when he got off at his stop, he kicked a soda pop can so hard it went clanking along the cement and pinged into a fire hydrant.

"How did school go?" his mother asked as always when she heard the screen door slam.

For a moment he thought of making up something interesting to please her, but he caught himself just in time.

"Oh, the same old thing," he said. How, he wondered, did she expect school to be, with no recess and writer's cramp from that "I must not tell lies" junk. And then, before he could stop his voice, he heard it blurt out, "Miss Lail hates me."

"No, Howie," his mother said turning from the sink where she was peeling potatoes. "Miss Lail may not like some of the things you do, but she likes you very much—just as she does your father and all her students."

Still, Howie wasn't convinced. Dejectedly, he headed toward his room. His world was just one big lump of misery, and nothing short of a miracle could change it.

On Friday morning Howie had what he thought was a brilliant idea. *He would take Friday to school with him.* Having the warm little body of the hamster next to him would be some consolation for all the rejections he was experiencing. After all, the two of them—the day and his pet—had something in common. They were both Friday. And besides, today was the day for Howie to get off restriction. He should be able to turn in his punishment

work to Miss Lail after school—he had worked on it last night until his hand almost fell off. Friday could help him celebrate.

Very gently, Howie opened Friday's cage and reached for his friend. He brushed off little bits of paper from his fur. Friday liked strips of newspaper for his bed. Holding him up, Howie took a good look at his fat little cheeks. As usual, Friday had stuffed them with the brown pellets of food from his bowl.

With Friday in one hand he searched in his closet for last season's windbreaker. It really wasn't cool enough yet to wear a jacket, but he would need it to hide his pet. The loose jacket would make the perfect maze for the agile little animal to scoot around in. Hmmm . . . the sleeves were short, but they would have to do.

Howie worked himself into the tan windbreaker and zipped it up. Then he lifted the band around his waist and slipped Friday underneath. His hamster inched his way in and wriggled around Howie's middle before he drew himself into a warm lump just above his belt.

On his way through the kitchen, Howie saw his mom eyeing his jacket. She reached out and felt his forehead. "Do you feel chilly, Son?" she asked. "I do hope you're not coming down with something."

"Oh, no Ma'am," he said, trying to make his voice sound cheery. "It may get cooler later on, and I just want to be prepared."

Howie left for the bus stop with his mother still standing

in the middle of the kitchen shaking her head. Sometimes he felt sorry for grownups. Life must be boring for them too.

He patted the warm little body through his jacket. Having a friend should add something to his day.

5
Friend "Friday"

Once he was in the classroom, Howie asked Miss Lail if he could have two rubber bands. She eyed him suspiciously. "They are not for shooting paper wads?"

"Oh, no, ma'am," Howie replied quickly, as if such a thing would never enter his mind.

At his desk he busily doubled them over and slipped them around the stretched bands at the wrists of his windbreaker. Even if Friday did sleep most of the day, he would probably get restless before school was out, and Howie certainly didn't want him running out of his sleeve and into the classroom. The very thought of it made him smile. He could just see Miss Lail jumping on top of her desk, and Carolyn screaming until her "boing" curls stood out from her head like the scream machine at the fair. As an extra precaution, he checked the zipper at his neck.

It was the middle of science class when Howie got up to trim his pencil that he ran into a problem. The grind of the pencil sharpener sent Friday into a frenzy. For a moment Howie thought he'd surely scoot right out of the neck of his jacket. He could feel the hamster's claws pulling at his shirt, and even his sharp little teeth jerking at the zipper that blocked his exit. Well, Howie would just have to forego getting up and going to the sharpener for the rest of the day, and that was going to be hard.

At lunch he waked Friday and sneaked him a crust of bread and a piece of carrot. Howie could feel Friday's little jaws moving as he chewed. When the hamster's ears twitched against Howie's underarm, he forgot himself and laughed out loud.

Fat Jake looked his way and with a mouthful of food mumbled, "Wonder what Whopper's got up his sleeve today?"

That struck Howie as so funny he couldn't even get mad at Jake for calling him Whopper. He thought how much he'd enjoy telling Jake what he really did have up his sleeve, but he could never give Friday's hideout away.

Tommy looked across the table as if he knew about Friday. Howie clamped his lips together in sign language. As Mamma Grace would say, "Mum's the word."

Suddenly a brilliant idea clicked in Howie's brain. Friday was a human recorder picking up signals and storing them in his cheeks. Once back at his computer base, Howie—now master programmer—would place his little intelligence wizard on a conveyer belt made especially for him. As Friday moved, the contraption would translate the coded message his body had intercepted into trade secrets. Howie could hear the top brass at the Pentagon heaping praise on the two of them. "Howard P. McDougal and his man Friday have cracked the spy ring, and in the process brought invaluable information to boost our country's place in the computer technology race."

Knowing good news is far more fun when it's shared, Howie gave a fleeting thought of telling Tommy his idea. But before he could make a decision, the jangle of the bell summoned them back to the agony of the classroom.

Once again Howie spent his recess writing, "I must not tell lies," but try as he might, he couldn't get through. Maybe he could sneak some more work on it during lessons.

His hand was already so tired that when Miss Lail assigned the written work in language, he couldn't work fast enough to have any time left over. Perspiration rolled down his face, but he couldn't take his jacket off. Besides, he was quite sure that Friday had relieved himself down the back of his shirt. It felt awful—and worse still, his mom would wonder about the soiled shirt when she did the laundry.

Nobody was supposed to be writing during reading period, so he dared not try. All he could do was watch the clock hands creep around. Worry was weighting him down. For some unexplainable reason he thought of the Tower of London and all the famous persons who had been imprisoned there. Then in some extraordinary way he became Sir Walter Raleigh, waiting in the Tower for his execution. Famous for his adventures in the new world, Raleigh was visited by many scholars and poets. Best of all, he knew he would never give up but would carry his visions to the bitter end. The strong spirit of martyrdom made Howie straighten up in his desk.

"Howard," Miss Lail's voice intruded, "when the three o'clock bell sounds, please remain in your desk."

With a sense of total desperation he marched his fingers across his desk top and off the side. He was no longer the valiant Sir Walter Raleigh; he was a mountain climber falling to his death.

"Now," said Miss Lail, when the room had cleared of the other students, "I phoned your mother that I would drop you by when you have finished your punishment work."

Howie let out a heavy sigh and pulled his yellow notebook from his bag. His freedom in the outside world seemed far away.

882. I must not tell lies.
883. I must not
884. I must
885. I must
886. I must

On and on he wrote—his hand aching. Several times he found Miss Lail looking at him with a peculiar expression. Now and then he looked outside. At this rate it was going to be dark when he got through. He might even be late for supper. Friday was really restless. He wriggled up and down inside the jacket. They hadn't gotten to celebrate Howie's freedom together after all. They'd only added to each other's misery.

And finally, when Howie thought he couldn't write another word, he wrote

1000. I must not tell lies.

He had made it. His notebook clicked as he took out the pages and straightened them up to turn in.

With her usual teacher face, Miss Lail took the efforts of Howie's week of work from his sweaty hands. While he watched, she began with number one and inspected each page to make sure he had not skipped any numbers. Then, placing the sheets in a neat stack on the edge of her desk, she picked up the pages one by one, tore them in half and let them plop into the trash can.

When she had done that, she dusted her hands together and said, "Get your books, Howard. I'm driving you home."

Under other circumstances he might have enjoyed a ride in Miss Lail's old black Oldsmobile, but he felt all icky, like he could get sick any minute. He did hope it wouldn't be in Miss Lail's car.

The ride was silent until Miss Lail pulled up in front of the McDougal home. Then she surprised Howie by turning toward him and looking over the rim of her glasses. "Howard," she said, "don't you think it's rather early in the season for that jacket you've worn all day?"

Then she reached over and patted the mound where

Friday slept on his shoulder.

Howie climbed out of her car with his mind whirling. How long had she known Friday was under his jacket? And more of a wonder—she had touched Friday, even if it was through his jacket.

Something smelled good as he opened the door.

"It's about time you got home," his mother called from the kitchen.

Howie detoured by his room and slipped Friday in his cage. "You'll never ever have to go to school again in your whole life," he promised. It had been a long, long day for both of them.

6
Killing Time

Howie usually felt happy on Friday evenings. Just knowing he didn't have to go to school the next day always perked him up, but this evening he was down. Even being off restriction didn't excite him. The day had just plain worn him out.

"Howard," his mother called. "Wash your hands for dinner. Your father and I are going to the Lackeys for dinner and bridge. I warmed you one of those TV meals you like with drumsticks and mashed potatoes."

Howie glanced out of the window. The days were already getting shorter. The sky had the haze it gets on autumn evenings. He'd wanted to ride his bike this first afternoon that he was free, but it would be too late by the time he ate. His parents had a strict rule about riding after dark. Even with flare lights that cars could spot, it was too dangerous, they said. And now a baby sitter, of all things.

"Well," Howie said, coming into the kitchen. "I'm not having a baby sitter. I'm keeping myself."

"The Lackeys' son Bob is coming over to be with you,"

his mom said. "You've seen him at church. He's a sophomore."

"He doesn't need to," Howie insisted. "I can take care of myself."

"I know you can, Son, but Bob likes TV and so do you. You'll be company for each other."

"Oh, well," Howie mumbled, "that's better than old Mrs. Perjerski with her knitting."

"And, Howard," his mother said. "I do hope you have learned your lesson about—" She hesitated. Howie had wondered when she was going to get around to *that*. How many times had she said "I can't bear *liars*." She even hated to say the word.

"Yeah, yeah," Howie said. "I know." He pushed his mashed potatoes up like Mount Vesuvius. The gravy puddled like lava.

"Miss Lail has been very patient with you, Howard."

Patient? Howie heard a voice inside his head scream. He jabbed the summit of the potato mountain and let the steaming liquid pour over the sides.

"It was sweet of her," his mother went on, "to take the time to stay after school with you today and then to drive you home."

"Sweet?" Howie heard himself bellow. "Miss Lail *sweet?*"

"What's all the yelling about?" Mr. McDougal appeared in the doorway, his red turtleneck shirt holding up a second chin. "What are you so excited about?" He put his hand on Howie's shoulder.

42

"Mom thinks Miss Lail's *sweet*." He made an effort to press his mouth around a wad of chicken.

Howie looked up just in time to see his father's expression change like magic.

"I'll have to agree with Howie," he said. "As well as I remember, that word does not fit Miss Lail. I believe the word martinet more nearly suits."

There his dad went again with those big words. "What's that?" Howie asked.

"A martinet is a strict disciplinarian." His dad rubbed his chin with his hand. "In fact, the only other time in my life that compares to the 'Miss Lail adventure' is my basic training in the Marine Corps at Parris Island." His dad laughed aloud. "I'd like to see that sergeant and Miss Lail buck each other."

"Miss Lail would win," Howie spoke emphatically. "She would flatten him with her stare."

"Oh, you men," his mom said. "At any rate, I'm glad both of you had the privilege of having her as a teacher, regardless of your biased opinions."

"We're sorry you missed her," his dad teased.

"Oh, she likes girls," Howie said, thinking with disgust of how Miss Lail doted on Carolyn.

His mom peered out the back door. "Here's Bob now," she said.

After welcoming the younger Lackey, Mrs. McDougal invited him to have a TV dinner with Howie. Bob said he had already eaten, so Howie watched while his mom showed Bob practically everything in the refrigerator, reminded him they would be at his parents' home if they were needed, and, best of all, announced that there was no bedtime curfew for that Friday night.

"But Howie," his dad said on the way out, "if you want to go up to Bakerstown with me in the morning to see some land, you'd better turn in before too late."

"What does your dad do?" Bob asked when his parents had gone.

"He appraises land but usually not on Saturdays." Howie shoved in his last bite, took a swallow of milk, and stuck his empty tray in the trash can under the sink.

As they headed toward the den and the TV, Howie answered Bob's questions about what grade he was in and who his teacher was.

"You got Miss Lail?" he asked, seeming to enjoy the fact. "She's a tough old egg."

Howie nodded. "You can say that again," he responded even though he wasn't sure just what Bob was referring to.

"She made me copy practically the whole *Thorndike Junior Dictionary* when I was in her class."

"What for?"

"Talking." Bob grinned. "I guess I used to talk a lot back then. Anyway, I got all the way to the *t*'s before the year was over."

"You're kidding." Howie started to mention the "I-must-not-tell-lies" thing but decided not to bring it up. It made him feel bad just to think about it.

"Nawh," Bob said, "I'm not kidding. I've still got it."

Howie thought about Miss Lail ripping his punishment

work to shreds. Maybe if he'd copied the dictionary instead, she would have let him keep it. He wished he had. At least he could have learned some new words. Then for some reason he didn't understand, his mind flitted to the expression on Miss Lail's face when she patted Friday through his jacket.

They settled down before the TV, and as far as Howie could figure out, he must have fallen asleep on the couch. He didn't even remember moving to his bed. The next thing he knew it was morning and his dad was waking him up to go with him to the country.

"Can I take Friday?" Howie mumbled in a sleepy tone.

"Better not, Son. He might get loose out there and you'd never find him."

"You and Mom said we'd get another dog."

"We will," his father answered in a way Howie recognized as not wanting to discuss it now. "But we want to make the best choice. You know how your mother feels about having a big dog, especially since you like for him to sleep in the house."

As Howie slipped into his shirt and jeans, he thought about the way old Chester used to snore. When he slept under Howie's bed, he would even wake him up snoring so loud. He remembered, too, how Chester used to drink water out of the commode. His mom hated for him to do that and drool water all over the bathroom carpet. It was fun going out in the country with old Chester. He would pad along behind them, wagging his tail and gathering up all the cockleburs in the field.

A second call got Howie to the kitchen, where his mom had ham and eggs waiting for them. Since both parents seemed to be in a pretty good mood, Howie made another stab at getting a dog.

"Bob said their cocker spaniel is going to have puppies."

Mr. McDougal stirred his coffee. "I believe I did hear that mentioned last night." He sighed as if in thought and looked at his wife. "That could be a possibility."

Howie's spirits lifted. A dog would be lots of company, especially now that he'd lost all his friends.

"If they're not all promised," Mrs. McDougal said, getting up from the table to get the napkins she had forgotten.

By the time he and his dad were on the long stretch of road toward Bakerstown, Howie was sorry he had come along. The ride was boring. He watched trees whiz by, dappling the sun in wavy patterns over his hands and arms.

Howie flipped the radio from station to station. When he did find a clear program, it was only a matter of minutes before it drowned out.

"That's because we're moving out of range of the radio transmitter," his dad said.

Howie tried leaving it on the garbled station and pretending the blending of voices and interference was a special code that could be unscrambled only when the trained ear found just the right frequency. But his dad kept reaching over to change stations, and before long, in desperation, he flipped it off.

When they finally did reach their destination, his dad

got out what he called a "plat" and spread it on the hood of the car. Howie looked too, until the heat from the motor got to be too much for him. He was hot and thirsty.

For what seemed like forever they plodded over fields and furrows dotted with scrub oaks, as his dad called them.

Occasionally Mr. McDougal pointed out markers to Howie, but all of it meant nothing to him. He wished he had stayed home. At least he could be riding his bike.

"Hey, Howie," his dad called. "Come see this centipede."

Howie jogged across the dusty earth without much enthusiasm until his dad said, "You know *cent* means one hundred, and supposedly this little creature has one hundred legs. That's where he gets his name."

"Gol-ly!" Howie heard himself say as he stooped for a closer look. And suddenly he thought of Tommy. He'd like to see the centipede.

"I wouldn't get too close," advised his dad. "I've heard the front fangs are poisonous."

Howie watched as his father picked up a stick and turned the fat-bodied worm over on its back.

"Look," he explained to Howie, "you can tell how he grows in segments. See. Each time another segment is added, he gets a new pair of legs. In fact, I think the number of legs they have determines their age."

"Then this one is old," Howie said.

"That makes sense anyway," his dad agreed, flipping the animal right side up.

Howie stayed behind and watched the centipede wriggle

along—drawing up and stretching out as it moved. What if, he thought, these animals could grow the size of dinosaurs and go into battle. They could carry a man on each segment and kill everything in their path with their poison fangs. Howie could just see an army of them going over the field toward enemy camps.

Then his dad called and, remembering how thirsty he was, Howie ran toward the car. On the way home they stopped at a roadside filling station for gas. They got frosted drinks from an old-fashioned cooler. Once Howie downed his and they were on the road again, it wasn't long before the hum of the tires against the road lulled him to sleep.

His mom had left a note for them on the kitchen table. She had gone shopping and they were to have the chicken casserole for lunch. Howie never could understand why his mom always had to mess up good chicken with all that other goop.

Afterward Howie was in no mood to accept his dad's invitation to run down to his office. He'd ride his bike to the park and just maybe he'd see some of the fellows from school and give them an opportunity to be decent to him.

7
Family Affairs

Howie's trip back from the country and his lunch "juvenated" him somewhat, as his dad liked to say but still it took lots of energy to pedal up the hill toward the park. Once there, it didn't take long for him to scan the area to see that no one he knew was there. Little kids played on the seesaws and the sliding board, while their mothers sat talking on nearby benches.

Howie pedaled on by the tennis courts. Balls pinged against racquets and thudded as they hit the court. He stopped his bicycle and rested one foot on the sidewalk. The happy squeals of children blended with the creak of the playground equipment and the hum of an occasional passing car. No one familiar there either.

He pulled down his kickstand, plopped down on the grass, and let himself fall backward. He closed his eyes and tried to remember the way it was when he and Tommy were together. It seemed such a long time ago. The sounds of the tennis court and playground came to him as another world separate from his. He opened his eyes to clouds shaped like a herd of buffalo. Beyond the darker mountain clouds, Indian hunters would be riding the buffalo to their deaths—arrows pointing in readiness.

With a sigh Howie pulled himself up and onto his bike for a whirl by the soccer field. A quick survey showed only screaming coaches and little red-faced boys trying their hardest to kick the spinning ball.

Back at home, the house seemed dead. Howie grabbed a drink from the refrigerator, flipped on the TV, and settled for an old Western he'd seen before. Dull old Ridgeville didn't even have cable TV. He could watch whatever channel he wanted on Saturdays, being an only child, but he sure wouldn't recommend it. Even if brothers and sisters fought, at least there was somebody to be with.

Before the movie was over, his mom came home and reminded him to clean "that rat's cage."

"His name's Friday, Mom." Howie's voice showed exasperation.

"Well," she said, "he is in the rodent family."

Howie took Friday's cage outside. In the other hand he carried a large jar with holes punched in the top for Friday to stay in while he cleaned the cage. He pulled some grass and dropped it into the jar for Friday to sniff over before he carefully slid the warm little body down into the glass container.

Clearing out the soiled paper, Howie made sure he left the pellets Friday had stored in the corners of his cage and enough of the old paper to make it smell like home. Howie used to shred the newspapers when he cleaned the cage, but he had learned that Friday liked to do that for himself. He also liked to arrange it in his cage in a certain way. Yes, Friday was an independent little hamster.

At first Howie hadn't understood how the jar of water hanging upside down outside the cage worked, but the man at the pet shop had explained that the water stayed in the container by air pressure. All Friday had to do was lick the drops of water from the end of the tube when he was thirsty. It also kept the cage from getting wet, for the store owner had told him hamsters do not like wet cages.

With the cage all fresh and clean, Howie returned Friday to his room. As he stooped to put him in his favorite corner, he spotted *Amazing Facts about Prehistoric Animals*. He had gotten it from his school library the week before all the hassle started and hadn't even looked at it. He fell across his bed and was soon caught up in the world of the tyrannosaurus, the stegosaurus, and the woolly mammoth. For the first time since he could remember, time sped by.

On Sunday when the McDougals worked themselves into a pew at church, Howie blinked his eyes in disbelief. Miss Lail sat slap in front of him, her back as straight as a ruler. He hadn't even known she went to Saint John's.

All during church Howie tried to think of ways he could get out of church without having Miss Lail see him. He thought of getting down on his hands and knees and crawling under the pews. But he could hear his mother asking, "Whatever happened to Howard?"

He could pretend he had to go to the bathroom and leave the service early, but Miss Lail would be on to that excuse.

When the sermon finally ended, Miss Lail turned to speak to his family. "And how are you this morning, Howard?" she asked in her stiff manner.

"Fine," Howie lied and for a moment he thought he saw a hint of a smile.

Once he succeeded in edging himself out of the church and to their car in the parking lot, he thought his parents would never come. He could just hear Miss Lail telling them all about the "I must not tell lies." They'd probably be mad with him all over again.

He took off his coat and tie and fell across the seat. He hoped she'd tell them how she ripped all his work to pieces right in front of his eyes, but he knew she wouldn't.

When it looked as if they were never coming, Howie got out of the car. How adults could hang around so long after church was over, he'd never know.

Hopping up on the low concrete wall surrounding the churchyard, he steadied himself and held out his arms for balance. He neared the cornerstone and paused. His dad had told him when the church was built they'd put letters and things in there and sealed them up like a time capsule. Hundreds of years from now maybe it would be opened. Howie would like to find a cornerstone made by the cave men. Maybe some day he'd be an archaeologist and dig in old ruins.

Much to his surprise, his parents were smiling when they headed toward the car. He wanted to ask if they had been talking to Miss Lail all that time, but if they were happy, he didn't want to bring up unpleasant things.

Once in the car, his mother looked at his dad and then at him. "Well." She smiled. "Miss Lail does—in spite of what you two think—have a sweet side."

Howie had opened his mouth to speak when his dad said, "She knows her business, if that's what you mean."

A sweet side! Oh, brother. Howie was about to pop to know what they were talking about, but he figured he'd better let well enough alone.

After lunch his mom ruined the rest of the day by announcing she'd like for him to go with her to the nursing home to visit Great Aunt Julia.

"I'm not going," he said in as emphatic a tone as he dared.

Then his mom came up with that sad "Chester look." "Oh, Howard, you can't imagine how much she would enjoy seeing you. Those old people rarely see young persons. It gives them such a lift, I'm sure."

"Well, I'm not going," he said so strongly that it got his father's attention.

"If your mother thinks you should go, then you'll go. A few minutes of your time for others won't hurt. In fact, it'll do you good."

"After all, Howard," his mom went on, "it is your Christian duty."

"Oh, all right. All right. I'll go. I'll go." His mom was beginning to sound like Miss Lail—duty, responsibility, and all that other junk.

At least the nursing home was just across town.

When they arrived, his mother said, "Come in and speak to Aunt Julia and then you can amble about the grounds.

I won't be long."

It had been such a long time since Howie had been to the nursing home, he'd forgotten how much old people look like withered cornstalks. Some of them hobbled about with canes. Others blocked the hallway with their wheelchairs. An old man with a stomach like a melon peered curiously at them as they passed and then moved crablike away. His mother smiled and spoke to all of them.

As they passed an opened door, Howie saw a man lying rigid in his narrow bed. He almost stopped in his tracks. He thought the man was dead. Then he heard him cough.

He was relieved when they finally did get to Aunt Julia's room. She was in bed, but she smiled and leaned up to hold out a shaky arm to Howie. "My, oh, my," she said, "what a fine young man you've gotten to be." Howie noticed her hands had little knobs at the knuckles and her skin was all covered with brown splotches.

"Yes," his mother was saying, "Howard is ten now." She laughed as if she was trying her best to sound cheery for Aunt Julia's sake. Howie couldn't help thinking she must have to work at that mighty hard because he sure was feeling low.

His mom was telling Aunt Julia how pretty she looked, but Howie wondered how she could think that. Her skin had worn so thin that her bones almost showed through and her orange-red hair sort of hung around her face, which had more splotches on it.

Howie was thinking Aunt Julia looked mighty bad, until he glanced over at the other bed in the room. The woman

54

in it was so thin that her head looked like a skull. Her eyes were sunk in bony cups.

"How's Mrs. Eldry?" his mother asked, nodding toward the corpse lady.

"Better. Much better." Aunt Julia's words picked up that same little cheery sound of his mother's. "In fact, her daughter left yesterday to go back to Virginia."

"That's nice," Mrs. McDougal said. "I brought goodies for you both."

His mother had sat in the only chair on Aunt Julia's side of the room and now Howie jiggled from one foot to the other—his restless signal that he was ready to go outside. He had almost given up on his mom noticing his message and was observing a peculiar-looking snake plant by Aunt Julia's bed when his mother said, "Howard, you may go outside while Aunt Julia and I visit."

"You can eat some pecans from the grounds," Aunt Julia said. "Not many folks here can," she laughed. "And thank you for coming to see me. You look like my side of the family, and it's always good to see family." She held out her wobbly arm again.

Howie was surprised at how weak and soft her hand was. The first time he had taken it, he had been concentrating on the splotches. Now he realized she had no more strength than a bowl of jello.

On his way out he moved around the wheelchairs in the hallway. A uniformed worker smiled and said "hello." In the lobby some of the residents waved at him and others stared as if he was from outer space.

Outside, he took a deep gulp of air and walked toward the pecan trees.

"Hey, fellow," somebody called.

Howie turned to see two old men sitting on a bench under one of the trees. "Come over here," he called. "I want to tell you something."

Somewhat hesitant, Howie moved toward them. The taller man wore farmer-type overalls. He was cracking nuts and handing the meat to the man beside him.

"He's stone deaf," the man pointed to his friend, who grinned at Howie. "He can't see too much neither—got cataracts so he can't tell the bitter from the nut. Now, take me, I got good eyes. But I don't have no teeth to chew nuts." He gave Howie a big grin, showing a snaggled tooth here and there. "So," he continued, "we just work together. I pick out nuts for him and he listens to me talk. Don't matter what I say, 'cause he can't hear me anyway." He laughed out loud.

"Oh," Howie said and thought how much that sounded like his dad.

"What I wanted to tell you is that when I was your age, I didn't think I was ever gonna get old."

"Oh," Howie said again. He watched the taller man hold out the nutmeat for his friend.

"Nope. But now I know that everybody—iffen he don't die first—is gonna get old. Yep. Some of them people"—he pointed to the nursing home building—"is in pretty bad shape. But me, I get along fine." He rattled on and on. All the while the man beside him kept a big grin on his face.

"Why, when I was your age I wrestled an alligator."

"You wrestled an alligator?" Howie plopped down on the ground in front of the men.

"Yes, sirree, I did. You know you got to watch out for their tails. Them rascals will whip their tails around and slap the daylights out of a grown man."

How, Howie wondered, could the old man be that happy out here. He must be bored to death. But he certainly hadn't led a boring life in the past. By the time Howie saw his mother coming out of the nursing home, he was engrossed in listening to a tale about the time the old man was bitten by a cottonmouth moccasin.

All the way home Howie repeated the stories to his mother. He tried his best to tell them just the way the man had, but he found himself adding just a little bit here and there. His mother really seemed to be interested. Howie could tell when her mind wasn't on what he was telling her. But this time she kept saying things like "Oh, my goodness."

Howie couldn't help thinking how much Tommy and the others at school would like to hear about the old man's adventures. But then he remembered that nobody wanted to listen to him tell anything anymore, and once again he felt down—really down.

8

Surprise

Monday morning Howie dragged himself out of bed and started dressing for school. Now that he was all through with that gosh-awful "I must not tell lies," his restriction from TV, and not being allowed to go out of his yard or ride his bicycle, he had only one problem—no friends.

No doubt everybody had gotten so used to not having him around that they didn't even think about him any more. All he would be good for was to give his former friends and classmates somebody to taunt. Worse still, the nickname of "Whopper" would probably follow him around forever like a bobbing tail.

He pulled on his jeans and let out a hard sigh. He would be like "Spit" in the story Miss Lail had read to them. The boy used to practice spitting all the time. He got really good at hitting his target and he could spit farther than anyone else. When his classmates thought of him, it was always as a champion spitter, so they started calling him "Spit." Years later, even after he was grown and had a family, the people he was in school with still called him

"Spit." The nickname spoiled a class reunion for him.

Howie guessed Miss Lail read the story to them so they wouldn't go around getting nicknames for themselves. Now he had gotten one anyway. It wasn't fair. Could he help it if he noticed things other people didn't? It would serve them all right if they'd gotten sick and died from the milk last Monday.

When Howie started out the door to the bus stop, he felt as if somebody must have come in the night and put lead under the soles of his shoes. His mom didn't even stop him on the way out to feel his head for temperature or anything. She was too busy getting ready to entertain her bridge club to even notice that he didn't eat all of his cereal. He sure hoped all the ladies would be gone by the time he got home—if that time ever came.

On the bus Howie ignored all the chatter around him and concentrated on the driver. He wore sunglasses, even so early in the morning, and the reflection of his eyes in the rearview mirror gave him a suspicious look. He kept jerking his head up for a panoramic view of his cargo, as if he were watching for something special, and then he would turn back to the road again. Once he looked long and hard down Lee Street, as if he expected somebody to meet him. Howie looked too, but all he saw was a clump of crepe myrtles and a Jiffy Mart. Nobody was even pumping gas at the Exxon station.

It took only one more of the driver's furtive glances in the rearview mirror for Howie to figure out what was going on. *They were being kidnapped—the whole lot of them.* He knew that sounded preposterous, but he had heard of that happening. He couldn't remember just where it had taken place, but the write-up had been in the newspaper. It had said a busload of kids had just plain disappeared and that parents and school officials were frantic. They had even called in psychics to help find out what on earth had happened. Some space fanatics thought the driver and kids had been scooped up in a flying saucer—one big enough to carry a school bus full of children.

For a fleeting moment Howie felt happy. Did they, he wondered, have school on other planets? He glanced around him. Some of the kids sat glumly, their bulging book bags juggling in their laps; others jabbered on without anybody even listening.

Well, he wasn't going to get into trouble again. He wouldn't tell them anything. Whatever happened couldn't be much worse than facing Miss Lail and a bunch of kids who didn't like him.

Howie's mind was still on how he could foil the kidnapping attempt if things turned sour when the bus screeched into the schoolyard.

When Howie passed the driver on his way out, he gave him a long, hard stare. It was hard to catch his facial expression behind those dark glasses, but at least Howie was on to his plans. Yes, this time he wouldn't spill the beans. He would just wait for "it" to happen. Maybe he'd even leave a note in his room at home for his parents to find—just in case. Then the skeptics would believe him the next time he warned them.

Howie didn't even bother to look for Tommy on the playground. He got by a group of girls huddled by the door, told the hall patrol he had to go to the library, and stepped inside. As he passed by his classroom, he saw a strange man standing by Miss Lail's desk. His heart lifted ever so slightly. Maybe they had a substitute. The man wore a red plaid shirt like one Howie had. At that moment he turned and Howie noticed he had a reddish mustache and crinkles in the corners of his eyes.

Howie took a step backward. That was when he saw Miss Lail. They couldn't be having a substitute with her here. She was looking at the strange man with a pleasant expression on her face. Obviously, Howie thought, she'd forgotten her rule of no smiles in her class.

In the library he turned in the prehistoric animal book and browsed along the shelf with the space books. Before he decided on one to check out, the first bell sounded. He'd better get moving. He couldn't take a chance on being late—not with things the way they were right now. Even before the jangle of the tardy bell died away, Miss Lail was settling the class. Without "wasting a moment," she called the roll and took the milk money, but for a wonder she didn't assign seatwork while she did it. During all this time the man Howie had seen earlier stood at the back of the room looking out the window. Howie wished he could do that. Even if his seat were by a window, he wouldn't be able to see out. He guessed the people who built this school put in high windows so kids couldn't have any fun.

Howie could tell the class was about to pop to know who

the strange man was, when Miss Lail finally stood up from her desk.

"Class," she said, "I have a surprise for you."

9

An Author to the Rescue

Howie felt everyone jerk to attention like soldiers saluting their captain. Miss Lail never had surprises. She believed in *making long-range plans, keeping on tasks,* and *working up to goals.*

Miss Lail's voice had more spirit than Howie ever remembered as she said, "We have a real live author with us today—someone who writes books—science fiction books."

Murmurs went up around the room and everyone shifted to look at the man, who turned from the window and crinkled his eyes at them.

"This," said Miss Lail, throwing her arm in his direction, "is author Richard Kirkland. He's in town visiting his mother and has graciously consented to come to talk to our class today." Then she "gave him the floor," as she liked to say, and sat down behind her desk.

Once again all eyes turned to the man at the window. They watched in disbelief as he reached up and snipped a green shoot from Miss Lail's hanging basket. Howie could

almost feel the gasps of breath around him. *Nobody* did
that to Miss Lail's plants—most especially not the one
she called her "hen and biddies" that had all those funny-
looking sprouts with more plants on the ends of them.
Howie always detoured around the octopuslike shoots.

Howie shot a glance at his teacher. She had not changed
the pleasant expression she seemed to have glued on for

the visitor.

In front of the room now Mr. Kirkland held up the tender green blade.

"What's this?" he asked.

Silence.

"Come on, " he urged. "What is it?"

"Miss Lail's flower," a timid voice offered.

"Yes. What else?"

"A biddy."

A slight giggle erupted. Students shifted in their desks.

He crinkled his eyes and waited.

"Trash," offered Tommy with a new boldness.

"And?"

"Chlorophyll," Carolyn said, and *ugh's* followed.

"You are all correct, but . . . "

They all watched mystified as the writer placed the green leaf shoot against one thumb and pressed against it. He blew and a keen little trumpet sound flitted over the room.

"Neato!" someone from the back of the room said and the class began to loosen up. Mr. Kirkland put up his hand for quiet.

"Now," he said, "the point I wanted to make is that you see in things what you look for. I saw music in that blade of green. And that's what we're going to talk about for a little while today. *What do you really see each day? Just how observant are you?*"

He paused and let the class think about his questions before he went on. "For starters, I'd like everybody to close their eyes. Right now. And no peeking. OK—hey, you there, close your eyes. Now call out the color of the dress Miss Lail is wearing today."

"Brown!" The cry went up in unison.

"Great! You'll make excellent writers. You're very observing."

A snicker escaped here and there. Miss Lail *always* wore brown.

"I don't want you to observe *only* with your eyes," he continued. "I want you to listen—really listen. I want you to think about all the senses God gave you—the senses of hearing and taste and touch and smell."

"All right now, close your eyes one more time. Let's see how observant your other senses are."

Silence.

"Call out what you smell," said Mr. Kirkland.

"Chalk."

"Oily stuff from the floor."

Howie found it hard to believe that this was really Miss Lail's class. She never let anybody call out an answer. You always had to go through this hand-waving routine and get permission to speak. Suddenly he couldn't resist calling out. "Feet," he blurted.

Everybody laughed and Howie opened his eyes. He saw Carolyn clap her hand over her mouth like she wouldn't dare laugh at such a thing. Howie wanted to see Miss Lail's reaction, but he wouldn't look at her for fear she was watching him.

For a wonder the author acted as if nothing had been out of order. "When I was your age—Miss Lail can tell you—" he looked toward her and back at the class—"I used to get into trouble."

This man was in Miss Lail's class!

"But you know . . . " He seemed deep in thought. "I think I might have learned something since then—something I can pass along to you to help keep some of you out of trouble and that will prove to be a lot of enjoyment as well. And that," he paused and then began to enunciate his words very carefully, "is the keeping of a journal."

"A journal?" Tommy asked with obvious doubt about the enjoyment part. "You mean a *diary*?"

"No, it isn't a diary. A diary records what you *do* each day. A journal records the things you *see, hear, smell, taste, touch*—that is, feelings, or anything having to do with you personally. Now—" his voice fell almost to a whisper as if he was telling a deep, dark secret, "best of all, a journal is a private kind of writing. Nobody sees your journal unless you choose to share it."

"Will it be for a grade?" Carolyn asked.

Leave it up to Carolyn to ask that, Howie thought.

"If Miss Lail wants to give you credit for writing in your journal, that's fine. But what I'm talking about is writing down things about people and objects around you that you observe—for yourself. Recording the way you react to happenings will really make you start to see the world you live in and to understand your own feelings better. And who knows, it might make you want to become a writer."

"Keep a notebook?" Jake asked in a disgusted voice and stuck out his tongue.

"Hey, listen," Mr. Kirkland's eyes gave an extra crinkle. "Don't knock it till you've tried it."

He waited for the laughter to end, and Howie watched Jake wiggle around in his desk.

"First of all," he continued, "look around your house and find an old looseleaf notebook—maybe one you discarded last school year. Then decorate the outside any way you like. Draw pictures on it, cover it with contact paper or whatever. You just need a book to collect your thoughts in. *But don't buy a new one.* There's something very comforting in old familiar things. Hey—" he said, walking down Howie's aisle, "just for starters take out a piece of notebook paper."

A couple of groans floated over the rustling of paper. Nobody would have ever complained to Miss Lail. But shock of all shocks, she didn't even move her hands off her desk. Her fingers remained locked together the way they had been since she first sat down.

"When you've prepared your journal, you may want to clip this page right into it," Mr. Kirkland added. "That's why I like the looseleaf kind."

Somebody got up to trim a pencil, but Howie sat still. This man had his curiosity up.

"Okay. Ready?" He paused and looked over the room that had quieted to see what he was going to do next. "I want you to make a list of the *ugliest* words you can think of."

"All right!" somebody said and giggles floated over the room.

"Okay," he repeated, putting up his hand for silence. "I haven't forgotten that Miss Lail likes an orderly classroom, and you know what?" His voice got down to the whisper stage again. "Being creative is one of the quietest processes in the whole world."

Howie sneaked a glance at Miss Lail. She was actually smiling, her lips drawn into a thin line.

"Now just a reminder." Howie thought Mr. Kirkland seemed amused at what he was about to say. "No profanity—just words that make your insides scrunch up when you think about them."

"Like *sewage*?" Howie heard himself ask.

"Yeah," the red-haired man shot back, "like *sewage* and *grime*."

Everybody took him at his word. Pencils scratched across notebook paper. Words came to Howie's mind almost faster than he could write them down. *Stink, soggy, buttermilk, castor oil, restriction.* He thought about *puke* but decided that might be *too* awful. Then he remembered the time he wrecked on his bicycle and hurt his knee. He wrote *pus* and *scab*.

Mr. Kirkland was right. His insides were feeling terrible, but it was not the same kind of bad feeling he had when he had write "I must not tell lies." This was a kind of fun bad. He wrote *belch* and paused briefly to think of his little new cousin whose mother "burped" him. He wrote *burp*, even though that was rather mild.

Howie was still going strong when Mr. Kirkland called time.

The class shared some words that caused noses to turn up and tongues to be stuck out. Nobody could believe how many Howie had thought of.

"OK," Mr. Kirkland said, "the purpose of that little exercise is to show you how words affect your feelings."

Howie had never thought about it before, but it was true. His insides felt all slimy. In fact, all the students' faces looked like they smelled something bad or had just seen a gruesome sight. Even the writer looked as if he was going to a funeral.

"On the other hand," Mr. Kirkland said, his face brightening. "I thank heavens we have pretty words in our vocabularies too—words that can fill our hearts with happiness." He walked up and down the aisle. "Now see how many happy words you can write before I call time."

"Oh," said a girl from the back of the room, "like *love*?"

Laughter, which Mr. Kirkland squelched with, "Exactly!"

Immediately the room became a happy place.

Howie's pencil raced: *snowballs, funny bone, summer, kites, swimming, jokes, bubbles, bicycle, scream machine, Friday, beach,* and on and on. Words came out so fast he felt like he was putting on brakes in his mind.

"Way to go, young man." Howie looked up to see Mr. Kirkland reading over his shoulder.

They shared words and then Mr. Kirkland asked them to start a new page for words that carry their own sounds.

Again Howie's pencil whizzed over the page: *buzz, crackle, clang, ping, rustle, growl, pop, slap, jingle, crunch,* and on and on. His hand didn't even get cramps.

"Now," Mr. Kirkland said, "once you get your journal set up, you can add to these lists all along. The main thing is that you see how writers work *with* words to make words work *for* them. We find just the word we want to make the reader feel a certain way—happy or sad, gloomy or scared or whatever. Or, as you see, we can make the reader smell things or hear them." His face really brightened before he added, "So if we choose our words wisely, we can really make the reader feel the same way we feel. Isn't that great?"

Howie liked this. Even as he continued to listen he added *plop* and *clunk* to his sound words.

Time sped by as Mr. Kirkland told them different ways they might set up their journals. Howie decided to make little tabs with Scotch tape to go at the tops of pages. That way he could get his thoughts organized into sections. He would label one section "Dreams." Boy, did he ever dream some weird things at night. He would put in the one about going to school in his pajamas. He might even write some of his daydreams down, too.

Another section, Mr. Kirkland told them, could be called "I Remember." When they thought of things they used to do as children, like playing "Red Rover," they could write them down. They could also, he said, write down the jingles they used to say when they played childhood games.

"Will someone tell us a rhyme for jumping rope?"

"Oh." Jan, who rarely said anything in class, spoke up. "I know one. 'Cinderella, dressed in yellow, going to town to see her fellow—'"

Howie couldn't remember when he'd had such a good time. Somebody else said, "We did 'peas porridge hot; peas porridge cold.'"

Mr. Kirkland laughed along with them. "You know," he said between chuckles, "you think you'll always remember these things, but you won't. And of course, class, what you're really doing with all of this writing in your journals—besides having a good time—is getting ready to write stories."

He paused, picked up Miss Lail's pencil container from her desk, and looked at it as he turned it round and round in his hand. "Just think of all the stories those pencils could tell for you if you used your imagination."

Suddenly he became very serious. "*But*, the imagination is extremely powerful and has to be used in the right way."

He laughed then in a strained sort of way before he said, "Actually, what I am about to tell you isn't funny. But, when I was your age—or somewhat younger—I used to get myself in some pretty terrible situations."

He walked back and forth before the class now as if he really shouldn't be telling them or anyone else what he was about to share. The smile had completely left his face. "You see," he said, "I really like to make up stories. I always have ever since I can remember."

He stopped dead in his tracks and let his eyes make contact with each person in the class—one at a time. Howie felt as if Mr. Kirkland was speaking right to him. "The only problem was," he said, "I told my stories for the truth."

"Why once," he went on, "I even told some pretty

73

important people my father was the captain of a ship and that we lived on the ship off the coast of Charleston."

"And you didn't?" Carolyn asked.

"Oh, no. I lived on Line Street right here in town." Then he brightened up. "But, things got so dull sometimes that I wished I could live somewhere else. I wished it so hard that I guess it actually did seem true." Howie straightened up in his desk. *Why, that was just exactly how he felt.*

"What else did you tell?" Jake asked.

"Oh." He smiled now. "I'm sure my mother and Miss Lail could fill you in on many of my tall tales. I don't remember lots of them because I didn't write them down, but folks got pretty upset with me. I can tell you that." He looked at Miss Lail and Howie saw her nod her head.

"Now," he said as if he were ready to change the subject, "I hope you will take keeping your journals seriously—even if you never turn out to be a writer. Keeping a journal helps you to be more aware of your world, *and* by *really* watching, listening, and thinking about others, you will understand people better and perhaps find out why they act the way they do."

For some reason Howie thought about the old people at the nursing home where Aunt Julia was. He surely under-stood better what being old was like since he had gone there. Maybe he'd go with his mom the next time she went. He might even want to write down some of the stories the man with the pecans had told him.

"Before I go," Mr. Kirkland was saying, "I would like to read you a story I wrote."

Howie wished he didn't have to go so soon, but in a few minutes he was caught up in a story about Eldred, a boy who won a trip to Mars by growing prize rhubarb in his garden. It turned out the Martians had been coming down every night and sprinkling dust from their planet on the boy's garden. They had chosen him to win the prize of a flight in space so they could get him to operate their project of growing rhubarb on Mars. Howie especially liked the way the Martians' space ship whirled down through the stars each night to the earth garden.

After that the author explained to them how he made up his characters for his stories by watching people. He told them he made Eldred look like his nephew, with unruly red hair, but act like himself as a youngster, for he had always liked gardening and had an interest in space. He knew exactly how Eldred felt. Howie could see that the people in his stories weren't any one person in particular but a blend of himself and real people he knew.

Before Howie knew it, Miss Lail was thanking Mr. Kirkland for coming and talking to the class, and he was telling them that he had to hurry to catch his plane back to Chicago.

"Before I leave," he said, "let me give you a final bit of advice. Try your best to do what Miss Lail asks you to do."

Howie couldn't help smiling. *Who dared not do what she said?*

Then the writer surprised Howie by stepping over and putting his arm around Miss Lail's thin shoulders. "Let me tell you," he said to the class, "if it had not been for this little lady, I'm afraid I wouldn't have had the discipline I need today to be a writer."

To the wonder of all, he leaned over and kissed her cheek.

Miss Lail followed him to the door and when she turned back toward the class, Howie saw a tight-lipped smile—the second one that day.

10
Howie's Journal

When Howie got home from school, he had one thing on his mind—finding an old looseleaf notebook and setting up his journal. In fact, he was so engrossed in the idea that he completely forgot about his mother's bridge club meeting at their house, until he saw the cars lined up along the road.

Oh, well, he'd work himself around to the back so he wouldn't be seen. He was even careful to catch the screen door before it slammed. Inside, he could hear the ladies talking in the living room. He certainly didn't want to get caught and have to say "hello" to all of them.

In his room Howie called a greeting to Friday, even though he couldn't see him. Obviously his pet had burrowed into the toilet tissue tube Howie had tossed in his cage that morning before he left for school. He could see where the hamster's sharp little teeth had nibbled away at the end of the roll of cardboard. He couldn't help thinking that wasn't too smart of Friday to eat up his own hideaway.

Howie dumped his books on his bed and all but stood

on his head as he dug into the jumble of junk in the back of his closet. Finally he came up with the notebook he was looking for. He fished in his book bag on the bed for the exercises he had begun in class. He'd liked doing the ugly words and the happy words and the sound ones. He clipped those pages in. Then he borrowed some clean paper from his regular school supply. Fishing in his bag again, he located a pencil, worked his shoes off, and dropped down across his bed. He wriggled into a comfortable position on his stomach and let his feet dangle off the side.

In bold letters he printed

JOURNAL

across the top of the first page. Below that he wrote

HANds OFF
WiTHOUT PERMiSSioN
of THE AUTHOR !

Keeping a journal was going to be neat. He'd cover his with Charlie Brown comics from the Sunday paper. As soon as the ladies left, he'd be able to get to the closet where his mother stashed old newspapers.

Stretching, he leaned over and pulled back his window curtain for a better view of their backyard and the silver maple. Dust motes floated in the yellow sunstreaks between him and the window. That would mean that at this moment he was breathing air that looked like that. He had never thought about it before. Mr. Kirkland had said, "Look—*really look* at things. *Listen. Smell. Taste...*"

Hmmm—Howie thought about food. Usually the first thing he did when he got home was get something to eat, but right now he was intent on getting his journal started without being seen by those ladies who would say how tall he was and all that junk.

He'd write a story—maybe one about Friday. Scooting backward and onto the floor, he edged near Friday's cage. He thought about how he had worked with his little pet, teaching him to climb on his shoulders and to find raisins hidden in his pockets. Speaking softly, he reached into the cage and coaxed Friday into his hand. He liked to watch him waddle along on his tiny hairy-soled feet, pausing now and then to sniff and listen. On occasion when Howie let him out, Friday would run along the baseboard of the room until he found the door. Then, quick as a flash, he would disappear. Howie remembered how upset his mother had been the time they couldn't find Friday for almost a whole day. He had escaped them by moving all around and ending up back in Howie's closet.

Yes, he would write a story about Friday and call it "The Little Escape Artist." Howie would be in the story too. He would be imprisoned, and unknown to his captors, he would have Friday undercover the way he had been in school. When his assailants left him jailed to die of starvation, he would bring out Friday and send him home. Friday's fat little cheek pouches, stuffed with bits of seeds from the strange area where the kidnappers held them, would be the clue to Howie's captivity.

Howie could see Friday now—gnawing his way out of the locked room and scurrying across fields and highways—sniffing his way home. Now and then he would move backward, the powerful muscles in his hind legs guiding his four-toed feet.

Finally, Friday would reach the McDougals', and Howie's mother would see the little golden hamster at their back door. Instead of yelling, "Howard, that rat's out again!" she would stoop down and scoop him up while she

called to Howie's father to come quickly.

They would put Friday on the kitchen counter, where he would sit back on his stub of a tail and "stand," as Howie had taught him. While they watched in consternation, Friday would push on his cheek pouches and expel seeds from the secluded place where Howie was being held.

At that moment Howie's mother—in real life—opened the door to his room. "Why, Howard," she said, "I didn't hear you come home. I was worried about you. All the ladies have gone and I wanted them to see you."

What she really meant, thought Howie, was that he didn't have on the TV and he hadn't messed up the kitchen. Quite frankly, he was a little surprised at himself.

Come to think of it, he *was* hungry. He slipped Friday back into his cage and headed for the kitchen. While he was eating leftover cheese straws and his mom was clearing away the dishes from her meeting, he told her about Mr. Kirkland's visit and the journal he was going to keep.

"Why, that sounds like a wonderful idea, Howard," she said.

When he told her about the story he was going to write, she seemed excited. "Oh," she said, "you can get your dad to make a copy for you at his office to send to Mamma Grace. She would really like that."

He was telling his mom about the sound words and listening for them about the kitchen when his dad came home.

"I'm bushed," his dad said as he dropped into his lounge chair. Howie had heard him say that before, but he had never thought about it. It really was an odd thing to say about yourself. He would put that in his journal too.

During dinner he remembered to smell his food and to think about how each thing tasted. He liked the way his butter oozed from his bread.

After dinner Howie found the funny papers and covered his journal with Charlie Brown as he had planned. Then he made tabs on the tops of the pages with little pieces of paper and Scotch tape. Behind "Dreams" he wrote about going to school in his pajamas and then he thought of the dream he'd had about the librarian at school. She'd had on a guard uniform and wouldn't let him have any books. Howie could see the science fiction books all lined up on the shelves waiting to be read, but he couldn't get at them. It had really been frustrating.

When his mom called "for the last time" that he had to get to bed, he turned in reluctantly. Lying in bed he listened as Mr. Kirkland had told them to do. His father must be reading the paper. Howie could hear it rattle like the crackling of a fire, and then there was a pop as his dad gave a section a special snap to turn it against itself. Now and then voices mumbled.

Finally, he listened to the house sounds. At first he thought it was quiet. Then he sharpened his ears to *really* listen. The refrigerator purred and clicked before its hum melted into the sounds of his parents' footsteps.

Down at the corner of their street a car revved into high gear. By the time it raced away, Howie was asleep.

11
New Lease on Life

The next morning it was all Howie could do to keep his shoes from galloping off in the thin autumn air toward the bus stop. Last week he had felt all icky inside when he even thought of school, but for a wonder he didn't mind it today. He was eager to see what the others had done about their journals.

He hummed a tune from a commercial and studied the scattered leaves that had already fallen on the sidewalk. He liked the way they crinkled under his feet. He did a high step and sent several scooting out of his path.

In his good mood, he even talked to the little kids who waited on the same corner.

When the bus lumbered up to their stop, Howie took a hard look at it. The color was really more orange than yellow, and mud had splattered over the wheels and up the side. Suddenly the long door swooshed open, just as if an invisible arm guided it. Howie watched as the hollow yellow creature gobbled up the little kids. He took a deep breath, straightened his shoulders, and stepped up to face whatever challenge lurked inside.

In his seat on the bus, he really listened. Every time the driver changed gears, the bus motor moaned and groaned like an old man climbing stairs.

He looked at the people around him. Mr. Kirkland had said to be a "people watcher." Across the aisle a little girl with pigtails clutched a pink lunch box with Care Bears on top. An older boy behind her leaned over and took a pigtail in each hand.

"I'm milking the cow," he said and looked around him to get a laugh. He got only a quick turn from the little girl who primped up her face and said, "If you do that again, I'm telling."

"Yeah," his seatmate said, "grow up, Punk."

Undaunted, the boy looked around him for other entertainment. For a moment Howie thought he would be the target of the boy's teasing, and he waited for a renewal of his nickname, "Whopper," but to his surprise it didn't come.

Well, even if it did come, Howie decided, he wouldn't let it ruin his day.

When the driver stopped for the railroad tracks, Howie noticed a fellow on the side of the road. He seemed to be waiting to hitch a ride. The way his cap was pulled down over his face made Howie remember the bus kidnappers.

Just as the bus was about to pull off, Howie spotted a dirty brown bag on the ground beside the man. A string drew the top of it into a tight wad. Howie thought he saw something wiggle inside. Was it a person? Suddenly he felt just like a private eye on television. He turned up his collar and scrunched his shoulders.

The bus bumped over the tracks and Howie's mind jolted. *Oops!* That was one for his journal.

His mind was still turning when his bus delivered them to school. In class Carolyn asked Miss Lail if people who had their journals could show them. Surprisingly, Miss Lail seemed pleased. She walked around the room looking at how creative the class had been in decorating the covers of their notebooks and held some up for the others to see. Tommy had drawn rockets all over his. Carolyn had done hers with pictures of kittens she had cut from magazines. Somebody else had drawn a big eye and an ear on his and another had contact paper with balloons on it. There was one with sailboats on wavy water.

Much to Howie's surprise, Miss Lail gave them free writing time while she took care of the lunch money and homeroom business.

Since Howie had his story about Friday all mapped out in his head, he started writing immediately. Across the top of his paper he wrote "The Escape Artist."

It was only right that the story be named after Friday, since he was the main character. Howie's pencil fairly flew across the page. He didn't worry too much about spelling. He would look up all the words he didn't know when he got home. For the time being he put a circle around the ones he was doubtful about. The plant book Aunt Marge had given him would come in handy to check the kinds of leaves and berries Friday would carry home in his cheeks. Showing a special kind would make a better story than just calling them plants and berries. Then, too, an author had to be careful. He couldn't name anything poisonous. Somebody might read it and think he could feed that to his hamster. Yep, the plant book would be just what he needed to add the final touch.

Howie was reading through his story to see how it sounded when Miss Lail called time. The next thing he knew Tommy was asking permission for Howie to read his story aloud.

As he stood before the class and began to read, Howie couldn't believe how eagerly everybody listened. They really wanted to know whether or not Friday would be able to chew his way out, pick up valuable clues, and find his way back home to save his master.

Mr. Kirkland had the secret all right. The class knew that what Howie was reading was fiction—that he had made it up—but they wanted to hear it. They seemed to have forgotten all about making fun of the things he had told last week. Best of all, nobody called him "Whopper."

When he had finished, Miss Lail said, "That's good, Howard. That's very good!"

Jake slapped himself on the side of the head like he wasn't believing that Howie had really written this story. And then Miss Lail began to clap and the class joined in.

Miss Lail approved of him! Howie couldn't believe it. Happiness flooded over him.

Suddenly his future flashed in his mind. He could see himself—a writer coming back to speak to Miss Lail's fifth grade. Maybe he would even stroll over to her hen and biddy plant the way Mr. Kirkland did and snip off a shoot. All the kids in the class would watch him in amazement.

Howie had known this day was going to be different, and he was right. It was turning out to be even better than he had hoped.

Carolyn read about a dream she had, and another boy read the beginning of a story about a bicycle race. Others had ideas they shared, and Miss Lail promised them some writing time each day.

Even when the class started reading from the science book, Howie was still happy in a private corner of his mind.

After he worked his story over with good spelling and better writing, he would get his dad to make a copy for Mamma Grace. His mom was right—Mamma Grace would really like it. And maybe if they got to go to Florida during Christmas holidays, he could write about some of the things down there.

Howie looked at the clock. He couldn't believe how fast time had gone by.

He knew his journal wasn't going to be any kind of magic wand. There would still be times when the clock hands would inch around the face. Some days would still be long and boring. But in spite of knowing that, he felt all sparkly and warm inside. He could imagine all he wanted to as long as he put it in his journal and called it fiction. That would be fun. But the warm feeling was there because he had friends again.

By break time Howie had already decided that his next story would be about his awful cousin Albert. He was always beating up on their little cousins at the family reunions.

He would have to change Albert's name. Mr. Kirkland didn't use real people but a mixture of those he knew. But that would be all right. Howie would still know the story was about Albert. He would have a fat lady—even fatter than the one at the county fair—sit on Albert. That oughta be good and funny, especially when Albert started coughing like a hawk with croup. Maybe that would teach him not to be such a bully.

He might not get to write his story today because he had Scouts, but he could keep it stashed in a niche in his mind. Anyway, Mr. Kirkland said everything in a journal didn't have to be completed. He said you called the unfinished ones "Works in Progress."

At lunch Howie's classmates were friendly. Carolyn, who had smiled the whole time he was reading his story, slipped down so Tommy could sit next to him. And to Howie's pleasure, his friends acted as if nothing had changed between them.

"You know," Tommy said around bites of French fries, "I ought to write a story about my cat. Old Tom really knows how to snoop about. He's not scared of anything or anybody—not even the devil."

"Just maybe," Howie said happily, "that's because he's kin to the devil."

"He's black all right," Tommy said, "black as the ace of spades. Not a white hair on him."

"It's too bad," Howie said, "we can't put Friday and old Tom in the same story, but I don't think they'd get along too well."

The boys around them were listening and Jake chimed in, "I'll bet you Friday can outrun old Tom."

"Yeah," Howie agreed, "but I wouldn't want to take that chance."

The remainder of the day passed far quicker than usual, and before Howie knew it he was on his way home from the bus stop, curled leaves crunching beneath his shoes.

Without even giving it a thought, he walked right by the Johnsons' house. Mrs. Johnson was in her yard. For a fleeting moment Howie thought she was shooing him, but then he realized she had a funny way of waving. He called back a "hello" to her. It was odd, he thought, how she didn't seem like such a "picklepuss" today. In fact, the whole world had changed.

A few spatters of rain swished across Howie's face, but not even that bothered him. Instead he thought about how the drops felt and listened for the sound of it about him.

Forgetting the weight of his books, he leaped over the low hedge along the edge of their lawn and let himself in the back door. On the table was a note from his mom.

Howie, I'll be back
from the grocery in time
to take you to Scouts.
Afterwards, the Lackeys
want you to come by
and pick out a puppy.
Love
M.